I0569905

Her Nutcracker Boyfriend

Love, Fey

PLUTO STREET
PUBLICATIONS

This is a work of fiction. Names, characters, places, and incidents are either the product of the author's imagination or are used fictitiously, and any resemblance to actual persons living or dead, business establishments, events, or locales, is entirely coincidental.

Her Nutcracker Boyfriend

Copyright © 2025 by Pluto Street Publications, LLC

All rights reserved. No part of this book may be used or reproduced in any manner whatsoever without written permission of the author except in the case of brief quotations embodied in critical articles or reviews.

Published in the United States of America
First Printing, 2025

No part of this work was created with the use of AI.

Cover Art by Love, Fey

Nutcracker Illustration by Amanda Webb
@LegendsofAukera

Dedication

To all the book girlies out there who count Clara and *The Nutcracker* as part of their origin story

To my very first nutcracker, who is on the cover and inspired the adorable illustration below, created by Amanda Webb.

To my writing bestie who had a gutter mind when I found a cute book for young readers about a nutcracker.

To little me who dreamed of being Clara. Although, little me, you should NOT be reading this.

1

"Strangest place you've ever masturbated?"

Robin was never good at these games. She wasn't adventurous or sensual enough to provide good answers. She was too safe, too shy, too *sweet*, as her best friend Livia would say. Her stories never warranted scandalized gasps or screeching laughter. None of her friends ever high-fived her or poured her a shot for having the juiciest response.

As her friends answered one by one, she tried to think of her own response, but she'd never self-pleasured anywhere but her own home, and nowhere interesting, either—her bed, of course, the couch, her desk chair. None of that was out of the norm. Definitely not with these girls.

"Front seat of my car, during traffic," Buffy said with a fling of her auburn hair off her pale shoulder.

"Girl, me too," Livia said. "I have one that you can sit and grind on. You can use it on any chair."

"I have that, too!"

Livia grinned at Buffy. "We drive home the same way from work and have ended up next to each other in traffic. The next time that happens, we're going to have an orgasm off. Windows down so we can hear each

1

other. First one to come wins. Loser buys the other a new vibrator. Their choice."

"You're on."

Kiki shook her head. Her brunette curls swayed. "The two of you are treading dangerously close to friends with benefits territory."

Livia leaned toward Buffy. Her black hair slipped off her tan shoulders, and the ends skimmed over Buffy's freckled thighs. "After she hears me come, moments before she comes undone herself, she may want that, and I'd be down." Livia's blue gaze lowered to Buffy's lap. "All the way down."

Buffy bit her bottom lip. Her cheeks were flushed now. Her eyes gleamed. "Stop," she whispered.

Grinning, Livia shifted back. "You won't be asking me to stop when I'm actually going down on you. You'll be beginning me *not* to stop."

"Okay, you two, back to your corners, you can flirt later." Kiki poured each of them a shot. "The strangest place I've ever masturbated?" Her amber gaze lifted toward the ceiling a moment. "That'd probably be the storage closet at work."

Robin's eyes widened. "Work-work, as in where we all work?" She rotated a finger in a circle to indicate the four of them sitting around Livia's coffee table that was littered with candy wrappers and bottles of booze.

Kiki nodded. "Yup. That storage closet."

"Were we at work at the time?"

"Yup."

Robin couldn't imagine doing anything like that where people were nearby.

Livia scooted closer. "And what prompted that?"

"Won't tell."

"Boo." Livia picked up a chocolate kiss and chucked it at Kiki. Then her attention shifted to Robin. "Your turn, Rob. Strangest place you've ever masturbated."

"Um. The tub." Robin shrugged. "But I wasn't taking a bath. I layered pillows and blankets and just..." Her voice faded.

Livia nodded. "A dry tub self-fuck is nice."

"Okay, my turn," Buffy said. "Hottest way someone gave you an orgasm?"

Robin didn't know. The men she'd been with had all done the usual techniques. None of them were into anything kinky or dark. "Pass."

"For that, you have to drink a shot." Livia poured her shot glass to the rim.

Taking the punishment, Robin downed the vodka.

"I've got a good one," Kiki said, "and I can tell you, without even hearing your answers, that I have you all beat."

Livia set her chin in her hand. "Go on."

"A remote-controlled vibrator."

The three of them exchanged glances.

"My boss had the remote control."

"Which boss," Robin, Livia, and Buffy shouted together. They had the same boss, and he had been the topic of many conversations and fantasies over the past few years.

Kiki only laughed. Then she nudged Robin. "For passing, you have to ask the next question."

Robin sighed. She never asked juicy questions, either. "Your first boyfriend or girlfriend?"

Livia smiled. "First boyfriend was a kid at my bus stop in elementary school. We had our first kiss there, too. *And*, in middle school, that's where I was fingered for the first time, while waiting for the bus to come."

"And *did you* come?" Kiki asked.

"Surprisingly, I did. First orgasm. He was really good with his fingers." She glanced at Buffy. "And so am I."

Buffy swallowed. Her cheeks flamed, and she cleared her throat. "First boyfriend...daycare. I was seven. We told our moms we got married at recess. First
orgasm...ninth grade. All the girls in my health class started sitting with our legs crossed, doing Kegels, and I came right there at my desk during a lecture about safe sex. Your turn, Kiki."

"My first boyfriend was in the sixth grade, who also happened to be my first girlfriend in the twelfth grade."

They all frowned at that.

"Lori transitioned in high school."

Livia nodded. "Nice. You're up, Robin."

Robin didn't look at them as she said, "This is going to sound crazy."

"Oh, finally something good." Kiki rubbed her hands together as if she were expecting Robin to share a scandalous tale. She was about to be disappointed.

"My first boyfriend was a nutcracker."

They stared as if she'd lost her mind.

"I was five or six years old and obsessed with *The Nutcracker* ballet. I had a VHS tape that I'd watch every day. Sometimes twice a day. I wanted to be Clara so badly, but I didn't know how to dance ballet, so I'd do karate to the music." She smiled as embarrassment filled her. "That Christmas, my dad gifted me a nutcracker. It was beautiful. Black painted suit and top hat, gold painted boots, and maroon poinsettias and green leaves along the hem and in the center of the hat.

"I loved that nutcracker so much that I'd dance with it while watching the ballet. I even tucked it into my bed at night. I had a special pillow to lay it on and everything. I called him my boyfriend." She shrugged. "As I said, I was like five years old."

"That is so cute," Buffy gushed.

"I love it," Kiki said.

"Her nutcracker boyfriend." Livia smiled. "Too cute."

They continued to gossip and drink until they decided it was late enough.

Robin requested a car using a ride-sharing app. She shared with Kiki, and the two of them left Livia and Buffy to do whatever they were going to do. At her house, Robin stumbled drunk to her curio cabinet. Through the glass, she gazed at her nutcracker. He'd lost his little white beard over his mouth that opened and closed with a level years ago, but his paint was perfect, and she still loved him. She opened the cabinet door and took him out. Her hand stroked over his silky white hair that brushed his shoulders.

"Still handsome," she whispered. "Come on, let's go to bed."

In her bedroom, she laid the nutcracker on a pillow, put on her pajamas, and flopped onto the mattress to sleep off the vodka she'd consumed as the loser of their game. She was always the loser.

Sighing, she laid a hand on her nutcracker. "Whatever. At least I have you."

She drifted off on a cloud of booze.

****

In the morning, something dug painfully into her cheek. Groaning, Robin lifted her head to see she'd been sleeping on her nutcracker and his little triangle nose had imbedded itself into her cheek. She rubbed her face. "Ow."

She picked him up and carried him to her living room where she stood him in the center of the coffee table. Drinking coffee and eating crispy bacon to cure her hangover, she stared at her nutcracker. "I can't believe I told them about you. I'm such a pathetic loser."

Sulking and still hungover, she dug through a box of childhood memories for her VHS copy of *The Nutcracker* and watched the program that she hadn't seen since she was a kid. Letting her inner child take over, she held the nutcracker in her hands and twirled around and around. Very ungracefully. Her laughter mixed with the classical music. After several revolutions, she staggered and dropped onto her couch, dizzy from spinning and feeling that vodka again.

Lying on her couch, with the nutcracker against her chest, she watched the rest of the ballet, wondering, and not for the first time, what it would be like to be Clara.

****

Livia visited a few days later and pointed at the nutcracker on Robin's coffee table. Robin had been enjoying getting back to her childhood crush, connecting with that little girl she'd been, and healing parts of herself that she'd buried long ago. She'd been dancing with the nutcracker every evening, talking to him, and bringing him to her bed. The truth was, the nutcracker comforted her, much like a teddy bear or a favorite blanket.

"Aw. Is this him?" Livia picked up the nutcracker. "For a wooden toy, I get it. Black suit, gold boots, white hair. Chiseled face and body. He's daddy material."

Robin snorted. "Only you would be bold enough to say that."

"Oh, come on, tell me you wouldn't rub your clit against his nose."

Robin gasped and took the nutcracker from Livia. "No." She eyed the nutcracker's tringle nose. Surely that wouldn't feel good.

"I've got you considering it. So much so that I bet I'll have you considering this...I dare you to fuck this nutcracker."

Robin's eyes widened. "What? No!" She glanced at the nutcracker. Horrified. She'd had it since she was a child. Doing anything sexual with it was out of line. "How would you even expect me to do that?"

Livia plucked up the nutcracker again, laid him on his stomach across her knees, and lifted the level from his back. Then she made a circle with her fingers and jerked her hand back and forth so that the level passed through the space in the middle of her curved fingers.

Robin snatched up the nutcracker. "I'm *not* doing that." Then she eyed Livia. "Would you do that?"

"Why not? Women have used stranger things to get off."

"Okay, well, not me. Vibrators, fine. Other inanimate objects? No."

Livia only grinned. "We'll see."

"We most certainly will not."

But that night, sitting on her bed, Robin couldn't expel Livia's dare from her mind. She examined the nutcracker and lifted the level. There's no way. Absolutely no way. Robin wasn't kinky enough or horny enough to try something like that. So, she plopped the nutcracker on her bedside table to stand guard rather than rest him on the pillow. Then she snapped off the light and rolled over so her back was to him.

2

C hristmas Eve, Robin sat at her work station, nibbling on iced cookies covered in sprinkles. Caroles played in the background, and her co-workers were laughing and chatting. The work day had ended an hour ago. Now they were all enjoying a little holiday fun, exchanging Secret Santa gifts, eating sweets, and drinking eggnog. Kiki had disappeared thirty minutes ago. And their boss was nowhere to be seen. Robin doubted that was a coincidence.

Parties weren't Robin's thing, especially not with coworkers, aside from Livia, Buffy, and Kiki. She'd rather be home right now, watching *The Nutcracker and the Four Realms*, curled up with her heated blanket, and sipping hot tea. But the Christmas cookies could stay. Christmas cookies were always welcome.

Livia propped herself on the edge of Robin's desk. "I have a gift for you." She held out a box wrapped with shiny poinsettia paper and a red bow.

"But we said we weren't going to exchange gifts this year."

"I know, but I couldn't resist. Come on." She set the box in front of Robin and used it to push the paper plate of cookies to the side. "Open it."

Robin unraveled the red ribbon, ripped into the paper, and lifted a white lid.

Nestled atop a cloud of tissue paper was a glossy piece of wood. It was thicker and rounded on one end and slimmed gradually to a smaller, smooth point. She frowned. "What is it?" She removed it from the cushion of tissue paper and dug the wider end to the back of her neck. "A neck massager?"

Livia laughed. "It's a massager, alright, but it's not for your neck." She lowered her voice. "It's for your pussy."

Robin dropped it back into the box and shoved the lid into place. "I can't believe you gave this to me at work!"

Livia waved her hand at the festivities. "No one is paying attention."

True enough. No one cared what was going on at her desk.

"You're going to go home tonight and fuck yourself with this dildo while thinking about your nutcracker boyfriend."

Robin gaped. "I can't do that." Her gaze flicked down to the piece of wood. "And not with that thing."

"Yes, you can. It's a real dildo, and it's safe. You won't get splinters or anything. It's from a reputable company, and just look at it. It's beautiful. Use some lube, and imagine it's your nutcracker's cock."

"Ssh." Her gaze darted around at their co-workers.

"The Christmas music is louder than our conversation. Relax." Livia laid the box on Robin's lap. "Go home, self-pleasure with this, and report back to me tomorrow."

Robin did go home.

She set the box on her dining room table, changed into fuzzy pajama bottoms and a long-sleeved shirt, and made a peanut butter and banana sandwich. She ate the sandwich with a glass of red wine and watched her movie. The whole time, she was aware of the wood dildo hiding in a box on her dining room table.

Halfway through the movie, her curiosity got the best of her. She paused the film and headed into her dining room. The lid lifted easily. The light-brown wood dildo was nestled right where she'd left it. She picked it up and studied the darker wood grain. It really was a beautiful piece, but she was expected to slip it into her pussy?

Her curiosity led her to the kitchen. At the sink, she ran the piece of wood under warm water and sanitized it with antibacterial soap before drying it with a paper towel. For some reason, she was jittering with nerves when she stepped into her bedroom, holding the wood dildo.

She lowered onto the edge of her bed. Her nutcracker stood there, right in the spot where she'd left him three weeks earlier. He seemed to be studying her with his painted eyes. Those black, flat pupils had a flex of white in them, a gleam that made it seem like he knew what she had in mind.

Holding eye contact with the nutcracker, she opened the drawer of her bedside table and removed a small tube. She squirted a line of water-based lubricant onto the dildo and used her fingers to coat the piece of wood up to where she'd grip it. Why were her fingers shaking?

"Okay," she said to the nutcracker. "I guess I'm doing this."

She picked him up from where he'd been standing guard and placed him back on his pillow. Then she rested her head on the pillow beside the nutcracker. Lying there, she slipped off her pajama bottoms and panties.

Biting her bottom lip, she slicked tip of the wood over her pussy.

She closed her eyes and tried to pretend the wood dildo teasing her was the hard, thick cock of a human-sized nutcracker, but it wasn't a man made of wood that she saw in her mind. A real man was there instead. He was clean-shaven like her nutcracker. White hair fell around his face as he hovered over her, but there was nothing old about this man. He was young and fit, and in his vast hand was a wooden dick, giving an all-new meaning to *woody*.

As she stroked herself with the dildo, she imagined it was the man with white hair moving the head of his cock between her vulva's lips. Up and down, using his penis to flirt with her pussy.

When she settled the head of the dildo at her entrance, she visualized the man pausing there, easing in just a bit, withdrawing, and slipping in a little more. Each time he dipped into her, he pushed deeper and deeper. Finally, she had the dildo in up to her fingers. Angling the dildo just so, she felt the smooth end rub against her internal flesh, but it wasn't her doing it. Rather the man in her fantasy was on top of her, working his cock in and out.

The touch awakened her nerve endings. Gradually, the sensations heightened, and she hummed with growing pleasure. She needed more, though, so she slipped her hand between her thighs and swirled the tips of her fingers over her clitoris. Instantly, her body contorted as her back arched, and her head knocked back.

She held that image of the white-haired man in her mind's eye while guiding the dildo and caressing her clit. More than anything, she wished he was really there doing those things to her. That he was the one filling her, touching her, with the sole mission to get her to come undone and shatter. Her yearning was so strong that her hand gripping the dildo became more vigorous, and she attacked her clit with faster strokes.

"Please." The word was on her lips. And it came again and again. "Please, please." She didn't know who she was pleading for or what she was pleading for exactly. Was she begging for her imagined nutcracker boyfriend to coax an orgasm out of her? Was she begging the universe to grant her this man? Maybe it was both, because she kept chanting that one word.

"Please…please…please…"

When she couldn't get a syllable out anymore, because all she could manage were moans and gasps, she thought it. *Please, please, please.*

As she thought *please* one last time, her orgasm flooded her entire body with sparkling warmth. It was so strong that her vision darkened and her body became rigid. After the orgasm faded, she lay in bed, stunned. She'd never given herself a release like that before.

Maybe it hadn't been her after all. Maybe it had

been the man she'd concocted in her imagination. The mere thought of him had been that strong.

Before she eased the dildo out of herself, she whispered once more, "Please." Still, she didn't know why she was saying it, except that asking, pleading, begging felt like the right thing to do in the moment.

Then she cleaned herself up and washed the dildo in the bathroom sink. She dried it with a fresh hand towel and carried it back to her nightstand where she set it next to her phone. Back in her panties and pajama bottoms, she crawled into bed beside her nutcracker.

Embarrassment rushed through her. At least she hadn't imagined her childhood nutcracker was the one fucking her. Still, the nutcracker had been there the entire time she'd masturbated. He'd been there, right next to her head, as her orgasm erupted from her. As weird as it would be to ever admit this, even to Livia, that action had connected her even more to her nutcracker.

Smiling to herself, she kissed his hard, painted cheek. "Goodnight."

3

obin rolled onto her side and cuddled against something solid. Whatever it was, it felt good. Comfortable. She nuzzled closer. She was drifting back to sleep when a sound met her ears. It was steady and soothing, like the sound of someone breathing. Beneath her hand, something lifted—a chest.

Her eyelids sprang open.

A man lay beside her, taking up half her bed with his large form.

She let out a scream and bolted upright.

The man sat up, too. He appeared startled. Scared. Worried. He lifted his hands, palms out, and opened his mouth, but nothing came out.

"Who are you?" She shoved away and pressed her back against the wall. In the darkness, she could see a shock of white hair that came to a set of broad shoulders. His face was constructed of a sharp jaw and thick dark brows, and he appeared more terrified than she was. "H-how'd you get in my house? And what the fuck are you doing in my bed?!"

"Robin…" His voice was a deep and strained rasp.

Hearing her name from a strange man's mouth,

who was in her bed uninvited, had her scrambling to the foot of that bed.

"Please…" He reached out to her, but she cringed back. "I won't…hurt you."

"Why are you in my bed?!"

"You…put me…here."

"No, I didn't. Who the hell are you?!"

"You never…" He cleared his throat and massaged his neck. "Sorry…it's strange. Talking is…strange."

Speaking sounded painful, as if his voice was sore.

"Who are you?!"

"I don't have…a name. You never gave…me one."

She frowned. "What do you mean I never…"

Her gaze shifted to the head of the bed and the pillow where his head had been resting. A black top hat lay there. She scooted toward it, avoiding touching the man with so much as a toe, and picked up the top hat. Her fingers traced the brim as she rotated it around. A gold silk ribbon at the base, and a large, dark red poinsettia with green leaves in the middle. It was her nutcracker's top hat.

She searched the pillow for her nutcracker, but it wasn't there. This man was there, instead. He wore a black suit jacket with more gold at the shoulders and at the cuffs. Gold buttons down the center gleamed in the moonlight that filtered through the blinds beside her bed.

Her gaze lowered.

A silk sash was tied around his middle, in that same brilliant gold.

She continued to scan him.

Black pants that hugged thick thighs.

16

Gold, laced boots that came up to his knees.

She covered her mouth. "Oh my God. You're...you're my nutcracker?"

He nodded. "Promise...I won't hurt you. I never...want to do that."

"This can't be happening." She dropped the top hat. "You can't be real. This can't be happening."

"But I am real, Robin." He cleared his throat again. "I don't know how. But I am. I'm real. And I'm yours, Robin. I've always...always been yours."

She swallowed.

He sounded so desperate for her to believe him, for her to claim him as hers. But she couldn't. This was just too bizarre.

"Robin. You're all I know."

She stared as her heart raced. "What do you mean? Were you...aware? As a nutcracker? Stiff and immobile, were you aware?"

"A-aware?" He peered off to the side as if contemplating the word. Then he met her gaze again in the darkness. "No. I was just wood then. A toy. But now, in this form, I have memories of every time you picked up me, held me"—he smiled—"danced with me. Those memories are all I know. You are all I know, Robin. Please, please don't be scared of me. Don't push me away."

Her heart ached. She couldn't deny that, and yet—

"But you can't be real."

"I am. I am." He curled his fingers around her wrist when she scooted away again. "I swear I am." Then he stilled, and his gaze lowered. She didn't know what he was looking at until his thumb stroked the inside of her wrist.

Her lips peeled apart. She watched his thumb brush her skin, back and forth. She held a shiver at bay.

"I...I've never touched you," he said. "I can recall you touching me, but I've never known what your..." His brows furrowed. "What is this?" He stroked her wrist. "This layer?"

"Skin."

"I've never known what your skin feels like. This...this is—" He inhaled. "To have skin and to touch your skin...I don't know how to describe..."

She knew. Without him having to say it, she knew, because she could feel it as he continued to skim his thumb over the delicate skin of her wrist. It felt intimate and like he was praising her skin with only his fingertips.

His worshiping stare rose up her arm to her shoulders. He lifted his hand from her wrist and trailed a finger down a lock of blonde hair. His eyes widened. Suddenly, he was shoving onto his knees and both of his hands were in her hair. She couldn't do anything but sit there and gape while he ran his fingers over and through the strands, touching them from root to tip.

"This is..." His chest expanded beneath his jacket, straining the fabric. "What is this?"

She blinked. "Hair. It's my hair."

"It's amazing."

His praise made her smile.

"I've never..." He rubbed the tips of his fingers together.

"Felt? What you're doing is called feeling. You're feeling my hair."

18

His brows lowered. "Feel. It feels—" Before he could decide what her hair felt like, he shifted to the side. "What was that?" His fingertips caressed the shell of her ear. "Soft. It's so soft."

She studied him as he massaged the edge of her ear. He was handsome. Like *The Witcher* with his shoulder-length white hair and face so chiseled that it made sense that he'd been made of wood. Except, *The Witcher* never gave off Golden Retriever vibes like this man was doing in spades. He was so eager, so innocent, and it was terribly cute. More, his attention was turning her on like never before.

His fingertips grazed the side of her neck, and with a curious eye, he skimmed his fingers to the back of her neck, making her shiver. His attention snapped back to her. "Am I hurting you? I don't want to hurt you."

"No. You're not. That was a shiver. That meant..." How to tell this man, who had become a man for the first time moments ago, that the way he was touching her was giving her sensations that he'd never experienced before? "How you're touching me feels good."

Now he was peering intently into her eyes. "It does?"

She nodded.

He redirected his attention to her neck. "Everything feels different."

"Texture," she said. "Different parts of my body, and yours, have different textures."

He tried out the word for the first time. "Texture." The corners of his lips quirked. "It's an odd word for something that is so lovely." Now he studied her again.

19

"Can I feel more textures?"

Enraptured by his curiosity, she took his hand and lifted it to her cheek. Then she glided his thumb over her skin.

His smile grew. "I like this spot."

"It's my cheek."

He studied her face. "And you have two?"

"Yes, just like you do."

He cupped her face with both of his hands now and rhythmically swept his thumbs across her cheeks.

She closed her eyes, relishing the attention and contact.

"How will I know if I'm hurting you?"

She kept her eyelids closed. "I'll flinch. Stop you. Say *ow*."

"Ow?" After a stretch of silence, he snatched his hands away. "You've said that to me before. And then you touched your cheek." He tentatively laid a hand to her right cheek. "This one."

It took her a moment to realize what he was talking about. Then she remembered waking up sleeping with her face on the nutcracker. "Oh, right. I was sleeping on top of you." She stilled. Having said that made her feel all sorts of awkward. "And...um...your little nose had...um...dug into my cheek."

"I hurt you."

"No, no." She shook her head. "It wasn't like that."

"I don't ever want to hurt you."

"Then you won't."

His thumb settled at the corner of her mouth. "You did something to me."

The pad of his thumb brushed over her lips,

causing her to suck in her breath. "You pressed these to my cheek."

"Lips," she whispered against his thumb that had settled at the bow of her mouth. "And it's called a kiss. I kissed your cheek. People do that to expression friendship and love."

"Do they only kiss cheeks?"

"No, you can kiss any part of someone's body, but the most common is another person's lips." Her gaze lowered to his mouth. He had a very kissable mouth. "Doing that…you're sharing something much deeper with someone. It's passionate and romantic."

He blinked.

"Do you know what that means? Passion and romance?"

"No."

"How is it that you know English but you don't know what certain words mean?"

"I don't know. I wasn't human until a moment ago."

She smiled.

Then his thumb cruised over her chin and down the length of her neck.

"What is passion?"

"It's a strong interest in something or someone. It's like a driving force."

"I have a passion for you."

She gawked. "You can't."

"Why not?"

"Because you don't know me."

"I told you, you're all I know."

"But that doesn't mean you know *me*."

21

His jaw flexed. He gazed at her shoulder as he skimmed his fingers over the curve. "You're wrong. I remember, Robin. When you were a child, you were so lonely. By yourself. Lost. Looking for…for…"

She could tell he was searching for a word to describe the deep yearning she'd endured as a child, but he didn't know what that word was. "A friend," she said as her eyes misted with tears. "I was searching for a friend."

"I filled that for you. I helped you."

She swallowed back her emotions. "You did."

"I gave you something, without being able to do a thing."

"You comforted me and gave me happiness."

"Even as you got older, I still did that for you, but it was different."

"Nostalgia. You reminded me of when I was a little girl."

"And recently, when you brought me out again, everything was…heavier. You were more lonely. More sad. More…" He gazed off, trying to decipher how to describe what he'd felt coming off her. "Just more."

She nodded. "Being an adult is hard. Being single is hard."

"Single?"

"Without someone."

"But you have me, Robin."

His earnestness made her close her eyes. The pressure squeezed out a tear.

He swept it away with his thumb. "What is this?"

She smiled, even as another tear leaked forth. "It's a tear. They're tears." She opened her eyelids to peer at him through the dam of water clinging to her eyes. "When people get emotional, they can cry. From happiness, sadness, even anger."

"And these tears?"

"I think it's sadness," she whispered. "Do you know about sadness?"

"I've felt it from you before." Then he jolted back. "I made you sad?"

She grabbed his hands. "Yours words brought out a little sadness in me, but it wasn't you. The sadness is from me, and how my life has unfolded since I was that little girl dancing with you in my living room. I didn't think I'd be alone."

"But you're not. And you never have been. You've always had me."

Her smile wobbled. "I guess I never realized that."

His fingers played with hers.

She watched him turn her hands over and skim his fingertips over her palms.

"More textures," he murmured.

"Yes." Her voice was a breath.

"I'd like to feel more. Please."

His "please" stole her breath.

"Okay." She considered where other textures were on her body. Taking his hand, she lowered it to her ankle.

His fingertips brushed the pale skin there before twiddling with her ankle bone. "What is this?"

"My ankle."

"It feels delicate."

"It can be, but it's strong and sturdy. My ankles can hold me up."

"Mm."

She was going to guide his hand to her knee when he stroked his hand up her shin. He made it to her knee his way and curved his hand to the back.

He ran his thumb over her skin. "You said 'I guess I'm doing this.' What did you mean?"

"What?"

"After you picked me up, before you laid me down right there"—his gaze shifted to the pillow—"you'd said 'I guess I'm doing this.' What did you do?"

She stole a peek at the wood dildo resting on her nightstand. "I...um...masturbated."

His brows furrowed.

"Self-pleasured?"

He didn't look any less confused.

"It's something people do when they want to feel good."

He peered into her eyes while sliding his hand over her knee to her thigh. "I want you to feel good."

She shivered.

"What do you have to do to self-pleasure?"

Oh my God, did he really just ask that?

"You touch yourself," she said.

"Like how I'm touching you now?"

"S-sort of, but there's specific, um, body parts."

"Which body parts?" He studied her. "I'd like to touch them all."

Holy shit.

She swallowed. "Well, this is one body part." And she brought his hand under her shirt.

He cupped her breast with his hand. "You have shapes."

She smiled. "Curves. You're touching my breast. I have two."

He stared at her shirt that hid his hand. It was as if he knew exactly what to do. His palm was vast and stamped over her breast, claiming it. His fingers squeezed gently. Then his hand shifted, and his fingers closed around her nipple, making her gasp. "What is this?"

"My nipple. It's especially sensitive. It can bring pleasure when touched *exactly* like how you're touching it."

"This feels good?"

The moment he asked that, she let out a moan. "Y-yes."

"That sound…?"

"Means it's very good."

He pinched her nipple softly, and she couldn't stop her body from jerking toward him and his touch.

"May I see?"

Turned on out of her mind, she didn't think twice and unbuttoned her shirt, revealing her skin. When she stripped her shirt off her shoulders, her breasts were completely exposed to him. Her nipples were hard peaks.

"They're lovely." Then he closed his hands around them.

She closed her eyes, allowing herself to sink into the sensation of him caressing her breasts with the most tenderest of touches.

Her skin tingled.

Her pussy heated, dripped, and throbbed.

When he pinched her nipples, she cried out.

"Do you know how I came to be like this? Like you?"

She opened her eyes and glanced at the dildo again. "I...I'm not sure." Surely masturbating with the wood dildo hadn't granted her nutcracker life. Right? Then again, sex was a powerful magic. Even solo sex.

He angled his head toward the nightstand. The next thing she knew, he was picking up the dildo and holding it in his large hand. "You keep looking at this. What is it?"

"It's a...um...it's a dildo. People with vulvas use it to self-pleasure. Last night, I used it. After...after I set you on the pillow."

He tilted the dildo from side to side, inspecting it. "How did you use it?"

Was she really going to explain the details for how vulva owners self-pleasure? Yes, yes, she was.

"I put it inside me."

His brows came together again. "Inside you?" He searched her face. "You mean your..." He pointed at his lips. "Doing that brought you pleasure?"

"Not my mouth. No. I have another hole. Somewhere else."

"Where?"

She pointed. "Between my legs. It's called a vulva or a pussy."

His gaze lowered. "May I see?"

4

Oh-my-everything-erotic-in-this-universe.

"You want to see my pussy?"

"I want to see every inch of you."

He had no idea he was requesting to see an intimate body part, a body part that was becoming hungrier and hungrier at his words, his stare, his touch. And she wanted him to see her pussy. So, she stripped out of her pajama shorts and panties. Then she laid back on her pillows and parted her legs.

He shifted between her thighs, making her bite her lip while he studied her. "Your pussy is beautiful." He lifted the wood dildo. "Putting this there was pleasurable?"

"Tremendously pleasurable."

"Can you show me?"

She blinked at his innocent question.

"I'd like to see what you did that gave me life."

Heart racing, she trembled with urges.

"Please."

She snatched the dildo and brought the wider end to her opening. Before she could slide it into herself, he grabbed her hips, making her gasp from his closeness.

"Don't hurt yourself. There's no way that can fit there."

She smiled at his sweet concern. "I won't hurt myself. Trust me. This…right here…" She swirled the end of the dildo over her pussy. "This is my vaginal opening. It stretches to accommodate dildos like this and penises."

His brows lowered.

"You have one."

"I do?"

"Between your legs."

He peered at his lap.

Her own gaze lowered. She was still stroking the end of the dildo over herself. The thought of him having a penis and wondering what it looked like coaxed a moan out of her, and she slipped the dildo inside herself.

His eyes widened. "Where does it go?"

"There's space inside." And she moved the dildo in and out.

His lips parted as he watched. "Doing that feels good?"

"Very good."

He was still grasping her hips, and he appeared rivetted by what she was doing. His gaze was locked on her while she fucked herself with her dildo. The fact he appeared unable to look away increased her desire. He had no clue about sex, had never felt pleasure, and didn't know a thing about a woman's body, but the way he gripped her hips and stared was intense and so incredibly hot.

She angled the dildo just so. The smooth end

stroked her g-zone. That pressure, that caress of the smooth wood against her flesh felt amazing. She lifted her hips, and his grasp tightened. "Jesus." His attention, his focus. She'd never witnessed anything like it before. Not by anyone she'd ever been intimate with. She watched him as he watched her. So incredibly handsome. So innocently erotic.

His chest rose and fell rapidly beneath his suit jacket. His lips parted.

She pumped her hips faster as her pleasure increased. The smooth end stroking her g-zone felt too good to stay still. And then there were his hands. His hands that continued to grip her hips even as they rose higher and higher. "Oh God. Oh God. Yes. Don't let go. Keep holding my hips. Please."

"I won't let go." His voice was deep, rough. It was the sound of a man aroused by what he was witnessing.

She cracked open her eyelids to see his chest heaving, his vision zeroed in on her pussy, sweat beading on his upper lip, and an unmistakable bulge in his pants. The size of it protruding beneath his belt sent a surge of pleasure shooting through her core. She tossed her head and arched her back. "Oh God." She jerked the dildo quicker. In and out. In and out.

His fingertips dug into her hips, and she could almost image that it was his cock plunging in and out of her pussy.

Heat flooded her core.

Sparks erupted.

And her pussy clenched around the dildo as she came. She cried out her release. Then she settled onto the mattress. Eyes closed, she tried to calm her heart and regulate her breathing.

After a moment, she realized his hands had disappeared. Fearing that he'd disappeared, that this orgasm could transform him back into a nutcracker, her eyelids sprang open. But he was there.

And he was rubbing his erection. "I had a...a reaction."

She stared as he stroked himself though his pants. "You were turned on while watching me. It's normal."

"Was I turned off before?"

She smiled, even as desire rushed through her. "It's a saying. You're aroused."

"Aroused. Yes. Yes, I'm aroused." His hand gripped the bulge, and he let out a groan.

She elevated onto her elbows. "Does that feel good?"

"Yes."

"I can make you feel better."

"How?"

Eager to give him pleasure, she scrambled onto her knees. Her hands shook as she opened his belt, unbuttoned his pants, and lowered the zipper. Nothing else was beneath his pants—no briefs, no boxers—so his cock sprang free. It was long and thick and veined, almost like the rings on the inside of a tree's trunk. So beautiful. So strong. And all hers.

She bent forward and swirled her tongue around the smooth tip. Around and around. The silkiness of his flesh there, at the head of his penis, increased her hunger, so she opened her mouth and accepted his cock into her mouth. She whirled her tongue around his girth, enjoying the texture of his hot, stretched, veined flesh against her hot, sleek, silky tongue.

"Robin." Her name was a gasp.

She inched back a little to suck on the tip.

"Oh...wow...I...I..."

The fact he couldn't form a coherent sentence and voice what he was experiencing had her smiling with his cock in her mouth. She hoped to teach him what to say in a moment like this. What she wouldn't give to hear him say "fuck."

She dove forward, taking his dick deeper. He tasted like oranges—from wood cleaner?—and margarita salt with a hint of cedar. He tasted damn good. "Mm." She bobbed her head faster.

He groaned.

Hearing that sound come from him, from something she was doing to him, from something he'd never had done to him before—he didn't even know what it was like to fist his cock into a frenzy until he shot cum all over his own hand—encouraged her to suck him harder.

"Robin." He moaned. "Robin."

His voice. Her name.

His pleasure. Her hunger.

Her lips popped off his dick when she reared back. She panted as she met his eye. "When I put your cock in my mouth again, I want you to grab onto my head. Pull me back and forth onto you. Fast. I want your cock so far in my throat, and I want you to do it."

He cupped her cheeks. "I don't want to hurt you."

"You won't. I want you to do this. I want you to—" She couldn't say *force her*, because she was begging him to do it. "I want you to bury your cock in my throat. Please. Please do that for me."

"Okay."

She dove forward, taking him deep into her mouth.

His hands tangled with her hair and formed around her skull. When she reared back, he dragged her forward by his hold on her head. The head of his cock bumped into the back of her throat, and she moaned her approval.

"Like that?" he asked while reversing her head.

"Mm-hm."

He tugged her forward again.

She relaxed her throat, opening it wider to accept him yet deeper.

"Robin…Robin…Robin…" He repeated her name each time he dragged her up his length. Her name had never been an erotic chant before, and hearing it now, on

this mysterious, sexy man's lips undid her.

She sucked on him.

"I…Robin—" Her name ended on a moan.

She lowered his hands from her head and leaned back to peer up into his eyes. Breathless she said, "You're close. You're going to come."

"You want me to go somewhere?"

She grinned. "You're going to stay right here, and you're going to keep on doing what you were doing. When I say 'come,' I mean an outcome to what we were doing. It's another word for orgasm. You're going to come."

"Where?"

"In my mouth."

He titled his head.

"What you're going to feel will become even more intense. Don't you stop. Okay? The moment you come, you won't be able to control it. A creamy substance will eject from your penis." She rubbed the tip of her finger over his slit and was awarded with seeing his eyes roll back at her touch. "Right here. And when that substance pumps out of you, it'll feel amazing." She held his hips again. "Don't you stop," she repeated. "Don't stop until you fill my mouth and throat with cum." Then she took him into her mouth again.

His hands instantly embraced her head, but he didn't move her up and down his length. He didn't need to because she was bobbing her head at a breakneck pace. God, he tasted so good and felt so good in her mouth. She was desperate for him to come so she could taste his climax on her tongue.

When he pumped his hips, lost in the sensation, desire rushed through her.

"Mm-hm." *That's it. That's it, handsome. Come for me. Please come for me.*

His groans escalated, growing louder and becoming more frequent. One right after the other. As his hips jerked with lightning speed, she met his movements with her own lunges.

"Mm...mmm...mmmm..."

More. More. More.

His body bumped into her face. "Robin...Robin...Robin..." Her name again, mixed with his moans. Then his cock jerked in her mouth and a gush of warmth hit the back of her throat.

She swallowed.

His body shuddered, and more cum splashed into

33

her throat.

He roared as he unloaded, and she drank every drop.

The moment his cock stopped bucking and his body quit shivering, she withdrew. Sitting on her heels, wiping her mouth with the back of her hand, she studied him.

His breathing was ragged. His eyes glistened in the moonlight. "That was…" He was breathless. "That was phenomenal."

"You know what phenomenal means?"

He nodded.

"You were perfect." With extra care, she tucked his depleted cock into his pants and fixed the zipper. "So utterly perfect." She stretched out on the bed and patted the place next to her. "Lie down next to me. Rest."

He dropped down and drew her into his arms. "*You're* perfect."

She cuddled into him and closed her eyes.

His fingers stroked her hair.

They lay like that for a long time. Not speaking. Just breathing and being.

She was drifting off to sleep when he said, "God."

Her eyelids opened. "Hm?"

"Is that my name?"

"What?"

"God. When you were…masturbating…you kept saying it. Is that what you want to call me?"

She lifted onto an elbow. "Call you? No, God is…" Best not to get into that. "No, I was saying that because it felt so damn good." She brushed a lock of hair from his temple. "What did you mean by 'is that what I want to call you'?"

"I don't have a name."

Robin blinked. Right, she'd never named him. Not like a child would name a baby doll or stuffed animal.

"Can you give me a name, Robin?"

Softening even more to this innocent man, she traced his jawline. "If you want me to, I will."

"I want you to."

"Okay." She considered what to name him. He was a nutcracker, but anything to do with that was obviously out. "Well, I'm not calling you Nut. Woody is a no, too. Let me think a moment."

Walnut.

Pine.

Oak.

No.

No.

No.

Almond.

Pecan.

No.

No.

All of those names were ridiculous. She couldn't give him a ridiculous name.

She thought back to her memories of him, of dancing and watching *The Nutcracker* with him in her arms. The ballet was about a young girl who was gifted a handsome nutcracker that comes to life. Together, they journey to the Land of Snow and the Kingdom of Sweets. The nutcracker didn't just become human. He was a prince.

A smile stretched her lips as she studied his face.

So devastatingly handsome. "How about Prince?"

"If you like it, I like it."

"I want you to like it for you, not for me. In *The Nutcracker*, when the nutcracker comes to life, he's a prince. Princes are regal and...people have named children Prince." She stroked his face with her fingers. "You *are* my prince."

He nodded. "Yes, I am."

"So...do you want that to be your name?"

"It already is my name."

She molded her hands to his face. "Remember when we talked about kissing?"

He nodded.

"I really want to kiss you right now."

"Please do."

She shifted closer. "There are degrees to kissing. I...I'm going to lay my lips to yours first. You can apply equal pressure back. Okay?"

"Okay." His warm breath blasted her lips.

She laid her lips gently over his. The contact was soft, tender, preparing him for more, because she badly wanted to do more, but she'd ease him in first with featherlight kisses. Turning her head slightly from side to side, she grazed her lips over his. The skin of their mouths tickled each other, and she shivered.

His arms contracted, and he pulled her closer, as if he could stop her from shivering. Except, that wouldn't be possible. She shivered because of him.

Touching her lips to his again, she applied a little more pressure, and he did the same. But it wasn't enough.

She inched back. "Now I'm going to place my lips

around yours so I can suck softly on your lips. Okay?"

"Yes."

She molded her lips around his, fitting them in just the right way so his top lip was between hers. And she sucked softly. She didn't have to tell him to do the same thing to her, because he did it without prompting. Still, she took it slow. A tender kiss to his top lip. Then to his bottom lip. Over and over until they sucked eagerly on each other's lips.

When he moaned, she shifted back.

He tugged her flush to him. "No."

She stroked his jaw. "It's okay. Now we're going to deepen the kiss. The deepest kiss we can possibly give each other. Do you want that?"

"Please."

"It'll involve our tongues."

"Tongues?"

She stuck out the tip of her tongue and pointed. "This." Then she licked the innermost part of her lips with just the tip. "I'll slip my tongue in your mouth, and you'll put your tongue in mine."

"And that will bring pleasure?"

"It will. Do you trust me?"

"With my life."

She leaned forward. First, she resumed kissing him like how they'd been kissing before she'd interrupted the mating of their lips. They locked their lips, sucking and tasting, before she spoke. "Open your mouth more."

His mouth widened. Once there was enough space, she dipped the tip of her tongue into his mouth so that their tongues met.

He jerked back as if startled.

"I'm sorry." Was French kissing too much for him?

Holding her close, staring into her eyes, he licked his lips slowly, as if testing his tongue's mobility and teasing himself with the contact. He shook his head. "More." His thumb stroked over her mouth. "I want more."

She latched her lips to his and probed his mouth with her tongue. His met hers instantly, and he groaned. That noise coming from him undid her in every way possible. She crushed her body to his and hooked her leg around his hip. His arms locked around her, his hands flattened to her bare back, and his fingertips dug into her flesh. That eagerness secreted a rich heat between her legs. God, everything he did aroused her.

She twirled and curled her tongue around his, stroked it, let her tongue dance with his in a slippery, hot tango that had her moans tangling with his.

His hands glided down to her butt. Warmth from his palms seared her skin with desire. When his fingers gripped her naked ass, she moaned into his mouth.

"You like that?" His question could've been spoken by a man who knew exactly what he was doing and saying, but he didn't. That didn't make it any less hot.

"Yes," she gasped.

He caressed her cheeks. "What is this?"

"My ass. You're groping my ass."

"Ass..."

"Butt is a more acceptable term."

"I like *ass*."

She smirked. "You're a little kinky, you know

that?"

"No, I don't know that."

She laughed now. "Well, you are."

"Do you like it when I'm kinky?"

"Mm-hm."

"Then I'll try to be kinky for you."

She bit her bottom lip.

His gaze lowered to her mouth, and he groaned. "More. Please."

They kissed with a hunger that ignited her.

His hands squeezed her ass, and she rammed her body into his.

He flinched back.

"What's wrong?" she asked.

"I want..." He swallowed. "What I'm doing here"—he rubbed her mouth with his thumb—"I want to do here." And he brought his other hand to between her legs, where her core throbbed for stimulation. "I want to kiss your pussy."

5

"Oh my God."

"Is that bad? Is that not allowed?"

"No, no, that's not bad at all and is very much allowed. It's called oral sex. It's like what I did to you. With my mouth. On your cock."

"Mm." His fingers stroked her.

She gripped him. "That feels good. That feels so good." She didn't want him to stop, but he pulled his fingers away and lifted his hand between them. Her cum covered his fingers. He rubbed his thumb over the creaminess, feeling it, making it swirl over his skin. Then he stuck his fingers in his mouth and sucked her cum right off. Watching him do that, her mouth parted.

Holy shit.

His gaze flicked to her. His pupils dilated.

In the next moment, he was shoving onto his knees, flattening her onto her back, and parting her legs. Then he bent down. Before she could even get a squeak out, his tongue lapped up her vulva. He did it again and again, as if he were a cat cleaning up cream from a bowl.

"Oh my God."

She went to grab his head, but he reared back before she could. "Is something—" She wanted to ask if something was wrong, but he cut off her words when he pounced off the end of the bed, gripped her ankles, and yanked her down the length of the bed.

A gasp flew from her.

He dropped onto his knees in front of her bed. His gaze roved over her from her right leg to her left leg. Seconds passed. After a moment, he threaded his arms through her bent legs and grasped her thighs. A growl left him, and he plunged in.

First, he laid his lips to her clit in a soft kiss and made his way down her vulva. Then he closed his mouth around her and made out with her pussy, using her labia as lips and her vaginal opening as a mouth.

She clutched his head. "Prince. Oh God. Prince, yes."

He feasted on her as if he'd never tasted anything as good, never eaten anything before. The fact was, he hadn't. Her pussy was the first taste he'd ever gotten. Not just of a woman. But of everything that existed in the world.

"So good," he said, with his lips on her vulva.

She writhed as he ate her so incredibly. Never had she felt anything so stunning, so complete. The moment he shifted his mouth and his tongue stroked her clit, she cried out. "Right there. Prince, please. Right there."

He focused his attention on her clit.

She arched her back. "Flick your tongue over that spot. Please, Prince."

He did exactly as she asked.

"Oh, fuck, yes." She hooked her legs around his

shoulders, tugging him yet closer. "Faster, harder."

He obliged with a groan.

Her thighs shook. "Will you do something else for me?"

He shifted back. His eyes gleamed with unmistakable lust as he panted. "Anything."

"Slip two of your fingers into my pussy. Right where my dildo was." She held up her hand, palm up, and curled her three fingers into her palm so her index and middle fingers were straight. "Inside, curl them like this." She crooked her fingers in a come-hither motion. "Can you do that?"

Rather than respond with words, he pushed his fingers into her pussy.

She gasped.

Right away, he massaged her g-zone exactly like how she'd instructed him.

She rolled her hips, matching the way he caressed her internally. "Put your mouth back—"

He fused his mouth to her and continued to stimulate her clit with his tongue. That, combined with his fingers awakening her g-zone, had her crying out.

Every flick of his tongue, every stroke of his fingers, increased the pleasure building inside her like a pool of shimmering sparks.

"S-suck on it. Pleas—"

She didn't have to plead, because he dove right into the task as soon as the request left her lips. He sucked so good on her clit that she saw stars. "Oh, fuck. Yes, fuck, yes." Her eyes rolled back. "Fuckfuckfuckfuckf—" A moan cut off her chant. "Oh, God. I'm going to come. Don't stop. Don't—" She couldn't say more while the sensations grew.

His mouth sucked harder. His fingers flicked faster.

Heat spread throughout her core.

Her mouth fell open, but nothing came out as a sequence of detonations erupted inside her. When the final one went off, a cry pealed from her.

He lifted his head. Meeting her eye, he withdrew his fingers and stuck them in his mouth.

"Oh God," she said, still shocked by the orgasm.

"Your pussy is delicious."

She smiled. "The bar is low considering you've never tasted anything else."

He shook his head. "The bar is high. Everything is going to have to taste better." He peered down as he palmed his erection through his pants. "I had another reaction."

"You're hard."

"Hard?" He grasped himself. "Definitely hard."

She sat up and grabbed his shoulders. "I want you."

"I'm already here."

She shook her head. "This is a different kind of need. It's a sexual need. I want you inside me." She laid a hand to his crotch. "I want this inside me. You recall how good it felt when your cock was in my mouth?"

He swallowed and nodded.

"And you know how it had felt with my pussy clenching your fingers just now?"

He nodded again.

"Then imagine how good it'll feel to have your cock inside me. Do you want to know that?"

"Yes." His voice was a whisper.

She studied him. Somehow, he still wore all his

clothes, even his tie. "I want to enjoy you. To do that, I need to remove your clothes. Do I have your permission?"

"Yes. You can do whatever you want to me, Robin."

"Jesus." She loosened the knot at his throat and dragged the black tie from his collar. Then she unbuttoned his jacket and worked it off his shoulders and down his arms. Beneath the fabric of his shirt, it was obvious how built he was. His muscles were unmistakable. One button at a time, she set about revealing his incredible body. Her fingers shook as they worked their way down his shirt. With each button she loosened, tan skin came into view. As the gap widened, his abs became visible. Abs that appeared to be carved from wood.

She parted the sides and gaped at his chest. Defined pecs. Abs that disappeared beneath the band of his pants. Cuts along his hips. Sculpted shoulders. Arms bulging with muscles. Forearms snaked with sexy veins.

"Holy shit."

Prince peered at himself. "Am I not to your liking?"

"Are you kidding me? Your body is impeccable." He had the kind of body born of fierce dedication. "I've never been with anyone as ripped as you are."

"Ripped?"

In way of explanation, she merely waved a hand in front of him.

"Are you second-guessing your decision to…"

"Have sex? No." She jittered while looking at his

body. "No. I'm not second-guessing a thing." And she removed his belt from his hips now. Then she unzipped his pants again. The sight of his cock made her shiver with anticipation. She tugged his pants down his thick thighs.

He removed her boots and stepped out of his clothes. Now he stood before her stark naked and sexy as hell. His cock twitched under her appraisal.

She laid her hands on his waist. "I want you on your back."

"Whatever you want." And he laid out in the middle of her bed.

That willingness sent a thrill through her. She scrambled onto the bed and straddled his hips. On her knees, with her hands on his vast chest, she met his gaze. "You're so handsome."

His hands flattened to the sides of her thighs. "You're so beautiful."

She ran her hands over his chest, feeling the dips and plains of his abs and pecks. "Are you ready for this? What we're going to do is going to be even more intense and far more intimate."

"I'm ready, Robin. I'm ready for you."

Her lips parted as her breath left her. She barely knew him, but at the same time, she felt connected to him. So much so that love surged inside her. Keeping her gaze locked on his, she guided him to her opening and lowered herself down, letting him fill her inch by inch.

His grip on her thighs tightened.

Once she was fully seated on him, she paused. "Are you okay?"

"Yes." His gaze lowered to where they were connected. "That feels incredible."

"Just wait." And she began to grind.

He was still staring at where their bodies met. His fingertips dug into her flesh. "Jesus," he said, mimicking her earlier response.

She grinned. How she wanted to hear him say that again. That and more. She kept the tempo slow and thorough as she rolled her hips, taking him in and out with a steady rhythm. His cock filled and stretched her so completely.

Staring down at him, she bit her bottom lip as her swollen clit rubbed against him with each forward motion. He was right. Him being inside her felt incredible. Was it possible that a man who'd been a nutcracker a moment ago had been made for her? Because she believed it.

His hands slipped up to her waist, and he grasped her. Having his hands there to anchor her, she quickened her movements.

His hips lifted, inadvertently thrusting deeper inside her, and she gasped. She bent over him to clutch his shoulders. In that position, her clit pressed even more firmly to him. Sparks detonated from the contact.

A moan broke free.

"Again," he ground out and tugged her forward.

Groaning again, she melted on top of him. She pumped up and down, faster and harder, striving toward that climax.

More sparks. More detonations. More moans.

"Fuck." That didn't leave her mouth. That came from Prince.

She reared back and pistoned her hips. Not just with the goal of reaching climax and having him fill her, but to hear him curse.

His own hips jutted off the mattress. "Oh, Jesus, fuck."

She grinned as she rode him, but soon, her own sensations became too intense, and she could no longer grin. Her mouth fell open, and a mixture of gasps and moans left her. God, he felt so good inside her. Every part of her glowed on the inside as her orgasm built.

Prince stared, clutching her hips, rearing up to meet her with thrusts of his own, and seething between his teeth. So damn sexy.

She pumped faster and faster. Her orgasm was right there. It was beginning. If she continued that tempo, it'd erupt, so she stopped.

Prince's brows furrowed. "What are you doing? Why'd you stop?"

"Because I was a second from coming, and I didn't want to come before you."

His jaw clenched. "What?"

"This is our first time. I didn't want to orgasm and leave you behind."

"Are you—" His arms wrapped around her. In a swift maneuver, he had her on her back. "Don't you dare stop because of me. Your orgasm is more important than mine."

She gaped, stunned by his statement.

He peered at their centers and stroked inside her. "Like this?"

"Yes." Her answer was a breath. "Just like that."

"Good. Now come for me."

"Yes, Daddy."

He titled his head while stroking again. "But I'm not your—"

"Ssh. Take me. Exactly like how you're doing it."

His pace quickened, and she moaned.

"You like this speed?"

"Yes."

He maintained that pace until she shattered beneath him with an orgasm that not only had her toes curling but her vision going dark.

A moment later, he came, too. The feel of his cum filling her made her quiver. She hugged him to herself when he collapsed onto her.

Her toes unclenched, and her vision returned to normal.

She rubbed his back. "Are you okay?"

"More than okay." His voice was a rasp in her ear that tugged her lips into a smile. "Can we do that every day?"

She laughed. "Maybe." But the reality that he would be a nutcracker in the morning came crashing down on her, and her heart broke in anticipation. "I have to take care of you. Can you roll off me?"

"Mm." He rolled onto his side, taking her with him.

She kissed his neck. "You have to let me go."

"Why?"

"So I can get up."

"You don't need to get up."

"Prince, I'm trying to give you aftercare following your first time."

"All right." He released her.

She headed for the bathroom.

"Robin?"

"Yeah?"

"You have a great ass."

She laughed. "I think I've created a monster."

In her bathroom, she picked up a hand towel.

"Do I scare you, Robin?"

"What? No. I mean, when I woke up and found you in my bed, yeah, I was scared, but you don't scare me anymore." She twisted the faucet to let the water heat up. "Why do you ask?"

"Because people are afraid of monsters."

"Not always." But she didn't want to explain monster romance yet, so instead she focused on wetting the towel until it was warm and rung it out. Then she carried it into the bedroom. "Here." She held it out to him. "To clean yourself up."

"But I like having you on me."

"Yup. Definitely created a monster."

He accepted the towel, wrapped it around his cock, and worked it up and down. His movements were slow, purposeful as he cleaned away her cum.

Shit. I can't watch that.

She picked up his discarded jacket, slipped it on, and fastened the middle button. Wearing his jacket and nothing else, she hustled to the kitchen. From the fridge, she removed a bottle of water. On her way back, she cracked the seal. When she stepped back into her bedroom, Prince was stepping into his pants.

The sight of him dressing caused her heart to stutter. "Going somewhere?"

He frowned. "I have nowhere to go."

"I meant..." She pointed. "You're putting your pants on."

"I was cold, and you're wearing my jacket, which..." He stepped up to her and skimmed the tip of his finger over her skin, along the edge of his lapel. "...looks really good on you."

She shivered when his finger tickled the side of her breast. "I...um...brought you water. You have to be thirsty after all that."

"Thank you." He accepted the bottle and guzzled half of it.

She cleared her throat. "You must be hungry, too. But..." She laughed. "...you've never had any food before. I guess pizza is a good place to start. Everyone loves pizza. Well, there might be a rare person or two out there who doesn't, but it's really good. Would you like to try it?"

"Sure."

She headed for the kitchen before turning back. "You can come with me. You're not restricted to the bedroom or anything."

"I'd love to be with you wherever you are."

She led the way into the kitchen. Each step she took, she felt him behind her. His presence reassured her, calmed her, but it also hurt her, because he wouldn't be there in this form for much longer. She'd be lonely again, and she didn't want to be lonely. Not after she got a taste of what having someone felt like.

Not after Prince.

6

I n the kitchen, she preheated the oven. When she turned, she spotted Prince in front of the curio cabinet.

"This is where you usually keep me."

She stilled. "Yeah. It is. I kept you in there to keep you safe. You are my most prized possession. Were...are..." She shook her head. "You're not a possession anymore, so...were."

He rotated and gazed at his surroundings.

"Are you okay?" She curled her fingers into the cuffs of his jacket sleeves. "I can't imagine how weird this is for you."

"It is strange, but having you here helps. You were always my vocal point."

"I can't be your everything, Prince."

"Why not? Isn't that what love is all about?"

She sucked in a breath. "Love?"

"Yeah." He erased the distance between them. "That can't surprise you, Robin." He wrapped his arms around her and held her close. "The only thing that I truly know is that I love you."

51

She stared at his chest so he couldn't see the tears filling her eyes, but a tear slipped lose and zipped down her cheek.

Prince's fingers curled under her chin. "Robin."

But she wouldn't meet his gaze. Couldn't.

"Did I make you sad again?"

"Not on purpose. This isn't your fault. This is me."

"What about me telling you that I love you made you sad? Isn't that supposed to make someone happy?"

"Normally, yes." She swallowed. "But you're not always going to be here."

"Where am I going?"

She finally lifted her gaze, but she didn't meet his. Instead, she stared at the curio cabinet and the empty spot where he had stood as a nutcracker.

He peered over his shoulder at it. "I can't fit in there."

"Not like this. No. But…" She lowered her gaze to the floor, unable to say it.

"But as a nutcracker I do."

She nodded. "We don't know how you came to be like this. Not for sure. And we don't know how long you have."

He picked her up, and her legs came around him. "Then we'll make the most of it." Peering into her eyes, he carried her to the counter and set her down.

She kissed him with the desperation she felt inside. The desperation conjured by her fear of losing him. Having him in nutcracker form wouldn't be the same. She'd miss him. *Shit*. He was brand new to her life and already she didn't want to be without him. Didn't want to imagine her life without him. Didn't want to lose him. She was terrified of going back to the way things were. Just hours ago.

It was ridiculous. This fierce longing. This irrational fear. Still, she couldn't deny it.

Maybe it was magic.

Maybe it was meant to be.

Maybe there was no way to explain what this was, but at least she could pretend, for the moment, that they had forever. In his arms, forever felt possible, magic could be real, and love could be attainable, which was something she never thought could happen. Before Prince. Before he came to life.

Their kiss spiraled out—all-consuming.

The oven beeped.

She leaned back, breathless and shaking.

His hands caressed her arms. "Are you okay?"

"Yeah. That kiss was…everything."

Forehead to forehead, he nodded.

"I have to put the pizza in."

He stepped back and assisted her off the counter.

She retrieved a frozen cheese pizza, topped it with fresh basil, sliced tomatoes, and a drizzle of olive oil, and placed it onto a rack in the oven. "Twenty minutes. Would you like to try wine?" Could a nutcracker-turned-man become intoxicated? "You could sip it. See how you like it."

"Sure."

She fetched the bottle of red she'd opened earlier that night and two glasses. In one glass, she poured it half-full. In the other, she added a splash for Prince to taste. They sat side by side on stools at the kitchen island.

"Here you go. If you don't like it, it's okay."

He raised the glass to his lips and sampled it.

She lifted her own glass to sip on the wine.

"That's good," he said, "but your pussy still tastes better."

His words startled her mid-swallow. Wine burned down her throat. She coughed hard as her eyes watered.

"Are you okay?"

She nodded while frantically tapping her chest. "Swallowed...wrong..." It took everything to get those two words out.

"That can happen? You can swallow wrong?"

She continued nodding.

He rubbed her back. "Do you need help?"

She focused on breathing through her nose to calm her throat. Finally, she got the coughing under control. "You'll have to hold any pussy comments while I'm drinking or eating. For my safety."

"I'm sorry."

"No." She laughed softly. "It's okay." She snagged a bottle of water from the fridge and sipped it to ease her throat. "I'm fine. Really."

"You're sure?"

His concern over her coughing fit was touching.

"I'm okay. Thank you." She stood beside him and looped her arms around his neck. His hands swallowed her waist. "I've never had someone care as much as you do, and you're so new to me. I'm not used to it, but I want to keep it."

"It's all yours, Robin. All yours."

She stamped her mouth to his and tasted the wine on his lips. When his hands caressed her body and

54

slipped beneath his jacket to cup her ass, she pried free of his intimate embrace. "Now would be a good time for us to talk and get to know each other." She resumed her seat. "But I can't ask you first date questions. Like…what's your favorite movie?"

He stared. Did he even know what a movie was?

"What's your favorite band?"

He didn't stop staring.

"Um…a band is a group of people who make music."

He didn't look way.

She smiled. "First concert, current job, favorite color—"

"I have a favorite color."

His answer surprised her. "You do?"

"Of course. My favorite color is the green of your eyes.

She blinked.

"And I may not have a favorite band, but I have a favorite sound."

She tilted her head.

"Your laughter."

"Prince, people would say you're obsessed."

His brows furrowed. "Obsessed?"

"All about me."

He gave a brisk nod. "They'd be right."

She smiled. "You are adorable."

"Is that good?"

"That's very good."

He reached for her hand, lifted it to his lips, and planted a kiss to her knuckles. "Why don't you tell me about your favorite movie, band, first concert, current job, favorite color? All of it. I want to know more about you."

"Okay, well, my favorite movie is *An Affair to Remember*. Deborah Kerr and Carey Grant meet on a cruise from Europe to New York, and their relationship is pure gold. Funny and witty, and just perfect. You know what? We should actually watch it tonight." She wanted to extend this night as long as possible. "Would you like to watch your first movie with me? As first movies go, *An Affair to Remember* is a peak cinematic choice."

"I'd love to."

"And while we wait for the pizza to get done, I can play you my favorite Lana Del Rey songs. But first—" She held up a finger. "I'll be right back."

With a plan in mind, she hurried into her room, selected a red sundress from her closet, and scurried into her bathroom. She washed up, slipped on the dress, pinned her hair atop her head, painted her lips red, and sprayed a bit of perfume on her neck. Then she cracked open the bathroom door. "Prince, come and get your jacket. Put it on with your shirt and wait for me out there." She stuck her arm between the door and the jamb, holding his jacket out and trying to stay hidden.

His tread came toward her, and his fingers touched hers as he took his jacket. When she released it and went to pull her arm through the gap, his fingers caught hers. Then his lips grazed the inside of her wrist.

"Prince." She clutched the doorhandle on the other side.

"I know. You want me to wait out there." He nibbled on the delicate flesh of her wrist. "I'm going."

But that was the thing…she'd didn't really want him to go at all.

His touch disappeared.

His tread left.

She rushed out of the bathroom to her bedroom door. Behind it, she called out. "Let me know when you're fully dressed."

A moment later, he responded. "I'm ready."

She retrieved her cell phone and tiptoed out of her room.

Prince stood in front of her lit Christmas tree, like a gift from the heavens.

As she approached, she hit Play on "Once Upon a Dream" by Lana Del Rey. When Lana sang the legendary opening of the song from *Sleeping Beauty* in her sultry, captivating voice, Prince rotated. He stilled immediately.

She continued to him, step by step.

"Red is my favorite color." The skirt of her red sundress swished around her thighs as she moved.

His mouth parted. His chest lifted against his buttoned jacket. "You're stunning."

She paused in front of him and laid her left hand on his shoulder. Her right hand she held up. "Do you know how to dance?"

He held her hand gently and braced the other at her back. "I'm a nutcracker. Of course I can dance."

And they danced to Lana Del Rey. First to "Once Upon a Dream," while rotating around her living room. Then to "Video Games." As they danced, she sang the lyrics to him. When the song "Summertime Sadness" started, she closed her eyes and willed tears not to form, because she hoped he'd kiss her hard before he left.

Their dancing slowed as Lana's voice surrounded them in a blue and purple cocoon of loneliness and longing and love. She squeezed her eyelids tighter.

Loneliness.

With him, she wasn't lonely.

Without him...

The oven beeped.

"I have to..." She couldn't say *go*, so she didn't say anything else and stepped out of his embrace to head to the oven. The heat from the oven blasted her face when she lowered the door, and she hoped it'd dry the tears in her eyes. Or at the very least give her an excuse for the warmth causing her eyes to water.

She took her time cutting the pie into neat triangles and distributing slices onto two plates. When she turned, Prince stood at the island, watching her. "We can eat this on the couch while watching *An Affair to Remember*."

"Okay."

She set the plates on the coffee table. "You might be more comfortable without your jacket."

Without question, he removed his jacket and draped it over a stool. He joined her on the couch. She passed him a plate, wondering if she had to explain how to chew, but considering he did well with drinking, maybe it'd come naturally to him. But she noticed him studying her while she bit into her slice. The curious look he gave her made her self-conscious. Still, she forced herself to chew and swallow and take another bite.

He bit into his own slice of pizza. Out of the corner

of her eye, she watched him closely, hoping he wouldn't choke. He managed just fine, though.

They ate their pizza and watched *An Affair to Remember*. Not long into the movie, he slung his arm around her and drew her closer. She cuddled into his side, with her legs curled beneath her. She couldn't help but think about how this time they shared together would be something she'd remember long past this night. This was truly an affair to remember. Even when the memory hurt. Even when the memory ripped her to shreds. Even when the memory became bittersweet. Even when the memory became…just a memory. With no pain. No emotion. No nothing. Because it'd be a memory of what she had and may never obtain again.

As the movie played, she grew tired. By the end of the movie, she could barely keep her eyes open.

Prince kissed her temple. "You should go to sleep."

She snuggled into his side. "I don't want to."

"You're tired."

"Are you tired?"

"I've been asleep until now, so no, I'm not tired, but I can watch you sleep."

"I don't want to sleep."

"Why not?"

She held onto him tighter. "Because when I wake up in the morning, there's a chance you might not be here."

"I will always be here." He glanced over his shoulder at the curio cabinet.

"It's not the same." She shook her head. "It's not the same at all."

"Come here." He lured her onto his lap until she

straddled him. Then he cupped her face with his hands. "I need you to understand something. Are you listening?"

"Yes." Her voice came out on a whisper as tears blurred her vision.

"Even when I'm not aware, I will always miss you."

When she squeezed her eyelids shut, her tears streaked down her cheeks.

"And I will always love you."

She captured his lips with hers and kissed him with every drop of loneliness she'd ever felt in her life. With Prince, she'd caught a glimpse of what life could be like with someone who adored her, and she didn't want to go back to her life before him. Why couldn't he stay? Why couldn't this be forever?

Prince stood as if she weighed nothing and carried her to her bedroom. At the edge of her bed, he lowered. "If tonight is really the last time we'll ever be together, I want to spend it with you here. In your bed."

The kiss they shared spoke volumes of goodbye. This was it. Their last chance. Their last kisses. The last time they'd make love.

Robin clutched him. This time, she would be making love with him. It wouldn't merely be a sex lesson. This would be an act of actual lovemaking because what she felt inside was too fierce to be anything other than love.

Love and desperation.

She kissed him with both.

Hands shaking, she undid the buttons of his shirt and guided them down his arms. Then she roamed her hands over his carved chest and abdomen. The dips and plains, the hard-packed muscle...every touch filled her with desire. She ran her palms from his shoulders to his wrists, feeling his biceps and the veins in his forearm. Jesus, he was exquisitely made.

She bent her neck to praise his body with her lips. Starting at his neck, with kisses to the side of his throat, she made her way to his wide shoulders, down to his large hands, back up to his collar bone, down to his pecks, then to his abs where she kissed each defined muscle, and lower still to the sexy cuts at his hips. Those she followed with the tip of her tongue.

Pausing at his pants, she worked open the zipper. "Lift for me."

He raised his hips, and she tugged his pants down to his thighs, exposing his gorgeous, engorged cock. She couldn't even finish removing his pants because she wanted his dick now. Gripping his hips, she bent over him and kissed the tip of his penis. Beneath her lips, his cock jerked.

A bit of creaminess leaked between her lips.

She shifted back to see a bead of pre-cum glistening on the head of his penis, pooling inside the crease. Her mouth watered, and she licked up that pearl of pre-cum while keeping her gaze on him.

His hands fisted into the bedding beneath him. A hiss escaped from between his teeth. Still watching, enjoying his reaction, she continued to tease the tip of her tongue along that crease, coaxing more pre-cum to emerge.

He groaned, and he was still groaning when she closed her mouth around him and let the head of his cock kiss the back of her throat.

"Fuck."

Up and down, she worked his cock with her gently closed fist and her mouth until his voice saying her name cut through her lust and his moans.

"Wait, Robin."

She pulled back.

He stared, breathing hard. "Your mouth is amazing, but I want to be deep in your pussy." He held out his hands. "Come here."

That was the second time he'd asked her to "come here." On the couch, it had been a tender request. In bed, it was a wanton instruction. Throbbing with needs, she scurried onto her knees.

"No, you come here. Sit on your heels like this." She showed him exactly how she wanted him to sit.

He tugged off his pants and got into position.

Clutching his shoulders, she climbed onto his lap. The head of his cock slipped over her wet pussy as she maneuvered into place. Legs on either side of him, with one hand to guide, she shifted closer. The head of his penis nudged into her, and she didn't stop until he was in as far as he could go. Locking her legs, she ground against him.

"Wait." He stroked his hands down her dress. "I want this off you. How do I take it off?"

"There's a zipper." She pointed to the back of her neck. "You'll feel a little piece of metal here."

His fingertips tickled her neck as he searched for the zipper. "I think I found it."

"Take it and drag it down. It'll open the zipper."

He followed her instructions.

"Now gather the skirt"—she wrapped her fingers in the fabric around her thighs—"and lift the dress over my head."

She lifted her arms when he drew the dress up.

He set the dress aside to appraise her. "Better." His gaze lowered to their laps.

She looked, too, to see the base of his penis. All the rest of him was inside her, filling her, stretching her.

His gaze flicked up to her. "Now."

That single word had her springing into action. She rocked against him. The entire time she did, she stared into his eyes. Tantric sex. She'd never done it, and the intimacy of it stole her breath. "You can...you can lift your hips, too."

As soon as she said it, Prince lifted slightly, testing.

She nodded. "When I roll forward, do that again."

She ground into him, and he gave a gentle thrust.

They moaned together.

"Yes, just like that. Don't stop."

Embracing each other to their chests, they held eye contact. Their movements were perfectly synced and so were their breaths. Prince's dick stroked against her g-zone, and his body rubbed against her clit.

What she'd been feeling inside up to this moment magnified to unbelievable heights. Not only pleasure, either, but every emotion. Overcome by it, she nuzzled the side of his neck and breathed in his woodsy scent that calmed and aroused at once.

Prince's lips trailed soft kisses along her shoulder.

Neither of them stopped the steady rhythm of their lovemaking.

Clutching Prince, with her fingers digging into

him, she moaned. Even though those moans left her, something else was filling her up. Something she'd never experienced before him, something she feared she'd never experience after him. She brought her lips to his ear and said it, so she could at least say it once in her life. "I love you."

Prince's gentle thrusts faltered and then stopped. He tangled his fingers with her hair. The grip was soft, but he still used the hold he had on her locks to pull her head back so that he could look into her eyes. "Say that again."

Tears bloomed in her eyes. She shook her head, although she didn't know why, because she planned to tell him again. She needed him to know before it was too late. "I love...I love..." She tried again. "I love you."

He crushed his mouth to hers. The way he kissed her screamed of the same desperation, plus something more—passion. She did her best to give him her love. He could take it with him when he left, and she hoped that someway, somehow he'd be able to feel it, even as a nutcracker.

She resumed the gliding motion, and he raised his hips. With their lips attached, their tongues slicking against each other, they made love with their bodies, with their intermingling breath, with their hearts beating against each other.

A moan tore from her, disconnecting their kiss. She wound her arms around his neck, buried her face in the side of his throat again, and hugged him while more moans escaped.

Prince's arms locked around her. His love

cocooned her. Every moan he released, she heard. Every breath he took, she felt. Every bang of his heart, reverberated through her.

"I love you, too," he whispered.

Those four words set her orgasm free, and she cried out with it.

Prince came as her muscles clenched him.

They stayed wrapped up in each other while his cum pooled inside her and their heart rates settled.

When their breathing calmed, Prince eased them to the bed, still inside her. His hands stroked her back. "Robin, if I don't live past this night, you have to know how much this has meant to me. You made my fleeting existence beautiful and magical. Thank you for every moment of this night. Thank you for…you, Robin. Thank you for *you*."

She knew what he meant by that. He was thanking her for sharing herself with him—her mind, body, and soul. She tightened her arms and legs around him. "Thank *you* for *you*."

And although she fought against it, she fell asleep in his arms.

7

Robin woke to a spear of sunlight slashing across her face. Prince's arms were no longer around her. She lay there, not wanting to get up and face the reality that she was alone. How could she resume her life after last night? How could she ever dare to dream of finding someone who could fill the void Prince left behind? What if she didn't? What if she never found love again?

Tears slipped from her eyes. One fell to her pillow, and the other collected at the corner of her eye, nestled by the side of her nose. She swiped it away with the tip of a finger. Sighing, she turned over and gasped. Prince lay there beneath the blanket. His bare chest was visible. His white hair was brushed away from the side of his face. That beam of sunlight that had lured her from her sleep stretched across his chest, directly over his heart.

Eyes wide, she rose onto her knees. "Prince, oh my God, are you alive?" She laid one hand on the center of his chest and the other against his cheek. "Prince?"

His eyelids opened, and his vision focused on her. "Hi, Robin."

66

"Oh my God." She cupped his face. "You're real?" She ran her hands down his arms now, needing reassurance that he was there and he was real. "How? How are you still here?"

Prince curled his hand around the side of her neck. "I told you, I don't know how I came to be. It was you, Robin. I'm convinced of that. Nor do I know how I'm still here." His thumb stroked her jawline. "Maybe it's because you told me you love me, and I told you—"

"And then I came. Just like when I was using the wood dildo and thinking about…well…you. I came, and it was glorious, and then you were here."

"I told you your orgasms are more important than mine."

Laughing, she pressed her lips to his. "I can't believe you're here."

He shifted her on top of him. "Don't question it. I'm here, and I'm yours. All yours. I will do whatever it takes to stay with you."

Those words dropped reality on her. This wouldn't be easy. He was essentially undocumented. The government would view him as illegal in every possible way and say that he shouldn't be in the country, be in the state, in her home, even in her bed. He didn't even have a last name. If they found out about him, they could take him away. When people were taken away, loved ones sometimes never saw them again.

Staring down at Prince, Robin decided right then that she'd marry him, help him apply for citizenship, and hire someone—or even teach him herself—so he could get his GED. Maybe Prince would have a knack for carpentry. Her uncle worked in construction and could give him a trade skill job if she asked. She'd do it all to make sure he wouldn't be targeted and could stay with her forever.

She grasped his shoulders. "I will do whatever it takes to keep you with me for the rest of my life."

He swooped her around so she lay beneath him. His cock was hot and thick between her legs. "Our life."

Nodding, she hooked her legs around him. "Our life."

He slid inside her as if to seal their promise.

She rose up to meet him thrust for thrust. Rather than a sweet loving making like last night, this one was frantic. Their bodies banged together, slapping wetly, as animalistic sounds broke from them one after the other. She shattered beneath him, and he pumped into her, drawing out her orgasm until he erupted.

They lay meshed together for a long time until Robin figured she needed to get them something to drink. "I'll be right back."

"All right." His fingers skimmed over her butt as she stood. "Bring that ass back to me so I can worship it."

"Definitely created a monster." She grinned.

"I'm *your* monster."

She'd never had someone want to be hers as badly as Prince did, and it left her stunned. The only thing she could do was get that water.

On her way to the kitchen, a knock sounded on the front door. She stole a glimpse through the peephole to see Livia standing there.

"Um. Hold on," she called through the door and

searched for something to cover herself with. She spotted Prince's jacket on the stool.

"Hurry up," Livia shouted outside. "It's cold out here."

Robin buttoned the jacket to cover herself. Then she scurried over and opened the front door.

Livia stepped inside. "Geez. It's freezing. You're lucky you're inside and"—she eyed Robin—"what are you wearing? Is that a men's suit jacket? And you're naked under it. That's a sexy look."

"Um." Robin hugged the jacket to herself to try to cover her curves. "What are you doing here? It's Christmas."

"I told you I would check in on your night with the dildo. How'd it go?"

"I thought you'd call."

"Where's the fun in that?" Robin tilted her head. "You've got sex hair and your skin is flushed. Were you just getting off with the dildo? I told you it's good."

Robin bit her lip. How exactly could she explain this to Livia?

"Robin, I'm cold without you in bed." Stark naked and sporting a hard-on, Prince stepped out of her bedroom.

Well, that's a good way.

His gaze shifted to Livia. "Oh, hi." Not an ounce of shame in his posture or his voice.

Livia's jaw dropped. She gawked at Prince and his erection. "Oh, hi, yourself. And who are you?"

Robin snatched up a fleece blanket from her reading chair and tossed it at Prince. He caught it and wrapped the blanket around his hips. It did nothing to hide the fact that he was aroused.

"I'm Prince," he said.

"Uh-huh. And how did you two meet?"

Before Robin could open her mouth, Prince answered. "We officially met last night."

"Really?" Livia gave Robin an approving wink. "Good for you."

Robin cleared her throat. "It's not like that." She laughed awkwardly. "Um…allow me to introduce you. Prince, this is Livia, my best friend. Livia, this is Prince, my nutcracker boyfriend."

Her Nutcracker Boyfriend

Love Fey

Author's Note

I got the idea for *Her Nutcracker Boyfriend* during a book buying adventure with my closest friend. At a local used bookstore, I found a cute juvenile story about a ballerina and a nutcracker. My inner child was delighted. I showed it to my friend, and immediately our minds went the other way. We talked about how Clara and *The Nutcracker* showed up on quite a few author's and reader's origin story posts on social media. Plus, I'd just purchased a smutty story about a door coming to life, so why not a nutcracker? We asked ourselves that, and my fate was sealed. I truly believe I was meant to write this innocently smutty story about a nutcracker coming to life, especially after I found this piece I'd written ten years before. It foreshadows this story in many ways.

A Nutcracker's Love

I was obsessed with *The Nutcracker* ballet when I was little. Every day for a year I watched an old tape and fantasized I was Clara. I didn't know how to dance ballet—except for standing with my heels together and attempting twirls—but that didn't stop me from showing off my moves…karate moves. I would jab my fists in the air and punch and kick as gracefully as I could.

Jab, jab, spin.

Jab, jab, twirl.

Jab, jab, hop and turn.

I was a karate-fighting ballerina in pajamas, a modern-day Clara.

For Christmas Eve that year, my dad set aside one gift. After all the other gifts were passed out and opened, my siblings and I looked longingly at the final wrapped gift. Who was it for? We all wanted it. We all wanted the privilege of opening the last gift that was special enough to be the grand finale.

My dad held it out to me.

My heart pounded with excitement, and I smiled with sheer delight. I peeled the wrapping paper off slowly, wanting to savor the moment. When the colored paper fell away, I saw a handsome nutcracker nestled in a box. He grinned at me through the plastic cover. His coat, pants, and hat were painted a shiny black. His boots, belt, and trim were gold. Hand-painted red flowers lined the bottom of his coat and sleeves, and a bigger red flower was painted in the middle of his tall hat. I had never seen anything more beautiful.

That night and for many nights after that, until the silky hair on the back of his head got matted, I slept with him in my bed. He had his own spot next to my pillow. I thought for sure that if he was close by while I slept that I would dream about the wonderful world Clara got to explore with the Nutcracker Prince.

I secretly thought of my nutcracker as my boyfriend. One day, he'd come to life and whisk me away to a happy life.

And when I played my old tape of *The Nutcracker* ballet, I finally had my own nutcracker to parade around with. I couldn't do my karate-dance moves, but I could hold my nutcracker like a baby and spin in circles. I could lift it toward the ceiling and mimic Clara as she fought to get her beloved toy back from her mean brother.

Every year after that, my dad gifted me with another nutcracker. Each one was lovely, but they paled in comparison to my first beloved nutcracker. Soon, I received nutcrackers year-round, whenever one was spotted at a thrift store or garage sale. Before I knew it, I had a collection, an army of nutcrackers.

I lined them up on my dresser. And then I'd rearrange them. Then I'd do it all over again. When I had more than could fit on my dresser, I lined them together on shelves. But no matter what order I put them in, my first nutcracker was always the first one in line, the one in charge, the one that had taken my heart.

Although, my nutcracker never became human, he was so full of life for the happiness he brought me. I still have him today. He stands at guard in a corner of my curio cabinet, keeping an eye on all. He's lost his little block feet, his triangle nose, and his beard that covered his mouth, but to me he is still as handsome as ever. He will always be my Nutcracker Prince, and I will always be Clara.

THE END

I hope you enjoyed that bonus content.

Until next time…

Love,
    Fey

About the Author...

Love Fey is author Chrys Fey's pen name for all the smutty romance stories her muse insists she needs to write. And who is she to go against her muse?

Each story is a spicy love letter to readers looking for book boyfriends and girlfriends of all kinds.

Fey's characters all have a bit of herself in them, whether that's her Arian fire or chronic pain. And every story includes something she loves—nutcrackers, Halloween, references to *Pride & Prejudice* and *Pretty Woman*, witches, gargoyles, and more.

She's a proud cat mama, a nail polish junkie, and will always write and publish romance no matter who may be against it. In fact, if a story idea may get close-minded individuals mad, that story moves to the top of her list.

Website:
LoveFey.com

www.ingramcontent.com/pod-product-compliance
Lightning Source LLC
Chambersburg PA
CBHW020638130626
46552CB00003B/1283